I0709279

The vampire king

Lucy Kean

Copyright © 2023 by Lucy Kean

All rights reserved.

No portion of this book may be reproduced in any form without written permission from the publisher or author, except as permitted by U.S. copyright law.

Contents

Angelina

Angelina knew that she had made the right choice of choosing Romania for her vacation; she felt that it was nice being away from Chicago. These past two years have been torture because of COVID-19, especially going through losses within her family.

Angelina's mom was a teen mother, and her father was some wannabe gangster who left after he found out that her mom was pregnant with her. Her mother gave birth to her to get welfare and other financial assistance. It didn't help that she quit school and would party. Angelina's maternal grandparents took her in so their granddaughter wouldn't have to be in foster care. They did their best to raise her; she remembered they always tried to buy her food and clothes and make small birthday parties.

Once Angelina was of legal age to work, she assisted them with the rent and bills. She did her very best in school; she wanted to give them a better life. Her good grades and test scores got me grants and scholarships; she was even accepted to the University of Chicago, making her the first in her family to attend university and graduate. She studied History and Archeology. Angelina remembered how her mom would always tell her that what she studied was worthless, but she proved her wrong when she was accepted into an internship in archeology in Europe. Angelina went on to impress her superiors throughout the years. Next year, she would become a full-time archeologist and be paid well.

However, last year, COVID-19 hit, and her grandparents contracted the disease. Angelina tried her best to care for her grandparents, but her mom would visit almost daily for money since she spent it on parties and drugs. Angelina's mother infected them with COVID-19; her grandparents died. This devastated the young woman, and their wish was for them to be cremated; they didn't want to burden their granddaughter financially.

Angelina's mom had no guilt and wanted what was hers in her parents' will. They left nothing to her; they said that she spent her inheritance. Angelina's mom disappeared from the face of the Earth; she was never seen again. The young woman moved to another apartment with her grandparents' ashes. It was their wish that they were to be scattered to their home country of Colombia. She wasn't ready to let them go and became depressed, but her acquaintances recommended that she travel once COVID restrictions lessened.

Throughout her time working and reading, Romania caught her interest. The country had many beautiful cities, towns, and nature. Castles were also popular in the country. Once the restrictions lessened, Angelina got my tickets; now, she was in the country.

It was her fifth day, and she didn't regret my decision. She could see castles, villages, cities, and restaurants and meet new people. Angelina was with a small tour group of ten people; they were all friendly people. The group was in a small tour van heading to the Hoia-Baciu Forest. While on the road, Angelina researched the forest, which had a lot of history. According to Google, there were legends about ghosts and disappearances. This was part of the tour package, and Angelina thought it wouldn't be fun if one didn't take a little risk.

Maybe she would see with her own eyes if the legends were true.

Hoia-Baciu Forest

The tour group arrived at their destination, the Hoia-Baciu Forest. It was the afternoon; the skies were cloudy. The tour group saw the forest, which had a strikingly frightening beauty. The trees were long and tall; there were a few bushes of different colors; leaves were on the ground as if welcoming outsiders to the secrecy of the forest.

Angelina couldn't get her eyes off the scene as she exited the tour bus. She thought it was beautiful with mystery."Alright, everyone, please gather around," said the tour guide. Everyone gathered around. "Alright, everyone, I will be your tour guide for this event. My name is Floran, and I am licensed to take tour groups to the forest."

"One needs a license? Why?" asked one of the group members.

"The forest is vast, and there are many pathways. There have been many missing cases and legends. This forest is referred to as 'The Bermuda Triangle of Transylvania.' Some legends say this forest is inhabited by ghosts, aliens, and even the devil itself."

Many group members mumbled to one another; Angelina was silent but felt anxious and excited.

"Now, if you follow me, I will lead you all to the safer path. Also, please walk together as a group. If one separates from the group, it can be easy to get lost in the forest." Floran began to lead everyone to a specific path to the forest. Everyone almost clung together except Angelina. She was at the back of the group, looking around the forest. She got her camera and took pictures and videos with her phone.

"The forest gained notoriety around the 1960s when biologist Alexandru Sift photographed a flying object in the sky above the forest. There was the disappearance of a shepherd and his 200 sheep who were never found again, and a five-year-old girl who reappeared five years later wearing the same clothes and without having aged even one day." Many tour group members shivered, but Angelina didn't seem too bothered. "There was the case of a missing woman who reappeared in the forest with a 15th-century coin in her pocket."

"Woah, are you saying that many people who reappeared from this forest could have time-traveled?"

Floran nodded. "Yes, speculations that this forest could lead to time travel."

"Hey man, getting lost here wouldn't be bad."

"You don't know where you might go or if you will ever return alive. The cases of many of these people were pure luck. Many people who were able to survive were never the same. Would you still take the risk?" Everyone was silent; Floran smiled. "Anyway, let's get a move on."

Angelina still walked apart from the group members. She silently stopped and wondered if what Floran said was true, especially about the time travel. That was when she thought of an insane idea, to venture out to the forest alone. "The forest is visible; it shouldn't be too difficult." She then walked to the left part of the forest, away from the path Floran led the group.

The silence and minimal visibility of the forest made her feel nervous, but she went ahead. It was nothing but many trees with similar and different shapes. The more she walked, the more she began to feel dizzy. The feelings were ignored; Angelina kept taking pictures and videos of the forest and herself. She stopped momentarily to look at the current video she had made, but there was something off when she looked at it.

The path was gone. She looked behind her, and the trail was gone. "What in the...?" Angelina walked back to where the trail was supposed to be and looked around. "Hello! Floran!? Anyone!?" There was no response. She ran forward, wanting to get back with the tour group. The more she ran, the more she felt that there was no end. Angelina stopped trying to regain her breath. Suddenly, the young woman began to feel a fever, body aches, and dizziness. She tripped on a tree trunk, making her fall to the ground and causing her to lose consciousness.

Hours went by, and Angelina slowly opened her eyes. When she did, she couldn't see anything. Angelina slowly sat up, looking everywhere. That was when she realized it was night; the starlight shone brightly in the skies, giving some light to the dark forest. "Hello! Anyone!?"

There was no answer. Angelina put her phone and camera away in her backpack. She slowly stood up and began to walk forward. "What was I thinking? How long was I unconscious?" The young woman began to regret separating from the group but hoped all was not lost. The more she walked, she heard a noise; it sounded like horses. Angelina stilled for a moment but thought there could be people if there were horses.

She began to run where the noises were heard; she then saw what seemed to be the end of the forest. It made her relieved. Angelina made it to the end of the forest. There, she felt relief and saw horses' reigns tied to tree branches eating hay. "Thank goodness. If only I could find the owners." Angelina saw the light from the corner of her eye and approached it. The closer she got, the more she heard men laughing and talking. "Ex-Excuse me; I need help." Angelina stopped in her tracks.

In front of her, there were a group of six men, but they looked different. All of them had long mustaches or beards. They wore clothing from the 15th century that confused her; the men also had long curly hair and swords. The men were silent, looking at her. Two of them spoke to one another about her clothing and appearance. Angelina could understand them, which was strange; not many people in Romania could speak English, but she didn't complain. "Sorry to bother you all, but I got lost in the forest and need help."

One of the men stood, sword at hand. "Who are you? Are you from the cursed Ottomans?"

"Ottomans?" Angelina was confused. In the history of Romania, the country was at war with the Ottoman Empire, but that was long ago. She couldn't understand why the man would bring an event from the past. "N-No, I'm from America, sir."

Everyone looked at one another. "What are you speaking of? Where is this America?"

"Uh, everyone knows what America is. It's another country far from here; it's not Turkey."

This confused the men more. "What should we do with her? She is speaking jibberish," asked one of the men.

"She could be a spy for the Ottomans; we cannot let her leave."

Angelina felt scared; she couldn't understand why the men were suspicious of her or didn't know what America was. That was when she remembered some of Floran's stories. Was it possible she was in another time, like many forest survivors? So many thoughts trailed through her mind, but she didn't want to find out.

"I believe we should take her to our Voivode. We don't know if she speaks the truth."

The young woman heard this. "Uh, that won't be necessary. I'll go back and find my way home."

All the men stood on their feet. "You shall come with us. Come with us lightly, or we shall use force."

Suddenly, Angelina ran back to the forest. The men got on their horses with weapons and began to chase her. Angelina tried to run as fast as she could, hoping she could return to her time. She screamed for Floran or anyone but could only hear the men and their horses going after her. They yelled at her to stop, but she refused.

One of the men got a bow and arrow aimed at Angelina's backpack. The arrow didn't pierce her skin, but there was force making her lose her footing. The men surrounded her. Two of them pointed their bow and arrow at her, while two others went to her, forcing her back to the camp where they tied her up and threw her onto a wooden cart.

"We should leave now; we don't know if she is a spy, and we cannot risk a possible attack. Let us go to our Voivode."

Travel

Angelina was scared; she didn't know what was going on. She was being taken against her will; her hands and feet were tied! Angelina was in a wooden cart being taken away from the forest. "I should have never separated myself from the group. The bright side is that I'm no longer in the scary forest."

She looked at the men; to her, they wore weird clothes. They seemed very old-fashioned. She didn't say anything because she didn't know what would happen. Everyone was quiet throughout the travel until they got into a dirt road. Night slowly turned into day, and Angelina was getting sleepy. She eventually let sleep take her occasionally, but it wasn't easy. The men would talk to one another about her and what she wore. It was as if they had never seen her type of clothes before. The young woman thought they were crazy but decided not to say anything. The men would make stops to let themselves and their horses rest. They would also hunt animals to eat. Angelina was getting a little more hungry, but seeing them slaughter animals made her stomach turn. However, Angelina couldn't deny that I was getting thirsty. She gathered her courage to ask them for some water.

Angelina was ignored; she got frustrated; feeling thirsty was the worst. "E-Excuse me! I want some water! I will not stop asking until I get some! Please!"

The men looked at one another. "She will not stop screaming and complaining."

"True." One of them came to me and gave me some water. It was cold, but it gave her more energy.

"Thank you, sir."

The man just looked at me, as did the others. Eventually, they continued until it got dark, and decided to camp. To her surprise, one of the men fed her food; Angelina ate without complaint. She didn't know where they were taking her, so eating as much as possible was best. "I-I need to go to the bathroom." The man looked at me, confused.

"What are you speaking about?"

"You don't know what a bathroom is?"

"Speak clearly, woman."

She took a deep breath. "I need to relieve myself. We've been traveling forever."

The man looked annoyed. "Very well, but you will be tied. I will not hesitate to cut you open if you even think about escaping. You understand?"

"Clearly."

Her hands were untied but motioned together in the front and tied again, but he connected a long rope. The man didn't untie my feet and ordered me to hop toward a treat; I felt embarrassed. Luckily, there was a large tree; Angelina went behind it, undid my pants, and did what she had to do. After she got herself ready, she was put on the cart again. They each took turns keeping watch.

Angelina accepted that it would be pointless, so she went to sleep.

It seemed like forever, but they were all on the road. When she woke, she saw what looked like a city from afar. "Thank goodness. I could get some answers, and maybe I could be let go." Angelina cleared her throat. "E-Excuse me, where are we headed to?"

"We will be taking you to our Voivode. He is there to keep his kingdom safe from the Ottomans."

"What are they talking about? Ottomans? Voivode? I did some reading and research about Romania. I remember that the Ottomans did invade and conquer some parts of Europe." That was when it hit her: the forest, the men, the Ottomans, and Voivode. "The forest! Was it a possibility that I time-traveled somewhere else!? I thought that those were pure myths to get more tourists! However, it makes sense why the men spoke and wore things they did! If I time traveled, which time did I go to?"

The young woman was so lost in thought that she finally realized they had made it to the city. Many people wore old-fashioned clothes; many buildings were made from wood or bricks.

Then, the men stopped, as did the cart. They were in front of a tall and more prominent building than the rest of the city. She was forced out of the cart, and the ropes on her legs were removed, but her hands were still tied. The men motioned her inside the building.

Once inside, there were flags, fire torches, and paintings of men and women; the walls were made of rocks and bricks. Angelina could hear men talking. When she walked deeper into the building, there were five long wooden rectangular tables where many men sat; their clothing looked to be of nobles.

When they all saw her, they became silent. Then, Angelina was pushed to the ground, and when she tried to get up, two of the captors pushed her down but motioned her to get on her knees. In front of Angelina was a long table with three men. Her eyes opened wide, and the man in the middle looked familiar.

"Wh-Who are you?"

Suddenly, one of the men hit me in the head. "Silence! You are before Voivode Vlad Dracul III!"

Angelina's eyes widened. "Holy hell! The man before me is none other than Vlad the Impaler!"

Vlad Dracul III

Angelina's eyes widened as she saw the man before her, Vlad Dracul III. "How can this be!? Is he the real Vlad the Impaler!?" Angelina asked herself. "No, I'm dreaming. All this is a nightmare."

Vlad noticed that Angelina had a light honey skin tone, long black curly hair touching her waist, and soft hazel eyes. She had an average body figure; her skin was clear and smooth that shined with the sun. Her slightly round face was youthful with a hint of maturity, showing bits of her age. She wore clothing he had never seen before. "Who is this woman?" asked Vlad sternly and commandingly.

"Voivode, we found this woman in the forest. She speaks with an accent and wears strange clothing. We didn't want her to escape, for there is a possibility that she may be an Ottoman spy," said one of the men.

Everyone in the room was silent as they looked at Angelina. Many were curious about the way she dressed and looked. "I-I'm not an Ottoman spy! I just got lost in the forest. All I want is to go home!"

"Silence! Do not speak without permission of the Voivode!"

Angelina looked up at Vlad, who eyed her with no emotion. "Are you Vlad Dracul?"

The onlookers murmured to one another. One of Angelina's captors kicked her in the back. She was shocked by the action. "Hey, what was that for? All I asked was a question. I don't even know where I am."

Vlad stood up and walked around the table before the young woman. "Speak your name."

"I'm Angelina, sir. Whatever these men say, I am not a spy or any-thing. Please believe me; I just got lost."

The Voivode put his hands behind his back, his eyes never leaving her. "Take her to my chambers. I wish to speak to this woman alone. All of you may continue with the festivities. We ride back home to Wallachia." The two men motioned Angelina to stand. They followed Vlad toward a pair of stairs leading to the upper part of the building. Fire torches lit the walls and structure.

Angelina noticed a single door. Vlad opened it, went inside, and motioned Angelina inside. "Unbind her, but shackle one of her hands to the wall."

The men did as they were ordered. They also left the room but were instructed by Vlad to stand outside. The two were alone. Angelina noticed how he stood at 5'9 tall. Vlad's face was slightly broad, with the signature long black mustache and a trim beard beneath his lower lip. His black hair was wavy, and the bottom tips were curly that went past his shoulders. What caught Angelina's attention were his light blue eyes. Even within the darkness, his pale blue eyes shined.

"Wow, you're good-looking in person," Angelina whispered. Vlad raised an eyebrow. "Oh, I'm sorry. I tend to speak to myself aloud without realizing it." She looked down, trying to refrain from blushing.

"Well, you are the first to speak such a thing. I was thinking of having my way with you, torturing you until your blood stains the floor. However, your words have made me in a better mood."

Angelina felt a chill go down her spine. The young woman remembered all the books and articles she had read about Vlad; he was ruthless. Vlad had a soothing and confident voice and appearance. However, there was a hint of secrecy and cruelty. His mannerism made it difficult for Angelina to gather whether or not he was being sincere or cruel. "I'm glad, sir."

Vlad chuckled while raising an eyebrow. "Hm, you hold no fear."

"On the contrary, sir, I am a bit. You are well-known everywhere, and you have quite the reputation."

The Voivode chuckled. Angelina thought he would hold more arrogance, but he didn't. "My reputation seems to have crossed the lands. Tell me of your home; you don't seem to be from my kingdom."

She debated whether or not she should tell Vlad where she came from. However, Angelina didn't want to risk being caught in a lie. "I was born far from here, sir. My parents abandoned me as a child, but my grandparents raised me. When they died, I began to work and travel independently."

"You still haven't answered my question, woman. Do you still wish to drag my question into the mud? I am not a patient man."

"He's more intelligent than I thought." Angelina sighed. "It's true that I'm not from here, sir. Would you believe me if I told you I am not from this country?"

"It is obvious. I am losing my patience."

Angelina sighed. "Would you believe me if I told you I am not from this time?"

Vlad stilled. "What are you speaking about?"

"I am from a country called the United States from the year 2022 AD. I crossed oceans to come here to travel. I walked to the Hoia-Baciu Forest and suddenly came here in your nation and your time. I don't know how in the hell it's possible, but here I am."

It was silent between the two. Suddenly, Vlad began to laugh hard and loudly. Angelina watched as she felt her hands getting sweaty. She waited until his laughs died down. "You jest."

"You said you wanted the truth. Tell me this. Why would I risk lying if you are smart enough to find out? If I lie, then you would torture me to death. All lies come to light, eventually." Then, an idea came up. "Look, I have my bag here. I can show you something to prove I am telling you the truth. Will you let me reach for it?"

Vlad went to her. "No, I shall do it." The older man looked at the bag; he was confused about how to open it. With Angelina's instructions, he eventually opened it. There were notebooks, clothes, snacks, and technology inside the bag. He took something out. "What is this?"

"It's called a Samsung cellphone, from my time. We use it to make calls, play games, and take pictures. We need wifi internet to make it work. Unfortunately, there is no wifi in your time."

Vlad pressed a couple of buttons, turning on the cell phone. His eyes held curiosity and fascination with the object. He saw the many apps and pictures as he slowly moved his fingers. "This is extraordinary. I have never seen such a thing."

"Do you believe me now?"

Vlad gave Angelina her phone back. "Hmph, it is still difficult for me to believe you, which is why I decided. You shall come to me to my palace."

Angelina gasped. "You're kidding?'

"What did you say?"

"It's a slang we use in my country. What I meant to say is, why? All I want is to go home."

"What I say is final. You shall come with my men and me to my palace. You have information that intrigues me. You shall sleep here. I cannot afford for you to escape. I will make sure that food is brought to you. Meanwhile, I have to be with the rest of my men." Vlad left the room, ordering his men to keep watch and to give her food while he was away.

Angelina stayed behind, stunned.

Thoughts

Vlad returned with the men and women celebrating, delaying the Ottomans' plans. He watched as everyone was eating and drinking. He found it pathetic that they celebrated for something inconvenient; the war wasn't over against the Ottomans.

Memories returned to him when his father, Vlad II, gave him and his brother to Sultan Murad II. Vlad bit his lower lip as he remembered when the Sultan and his council forced him and his brother, Radu, to learn the ways of Allah and Ottoman culture. Radu accepted the teachings that they were taught and welcomed the thought that Wallachia would benefit from the teachings.

As an adolescent, there were rumors that Radu was a concubine for Mehmed II. He didn't want to believe it. Vlad wanted to protect his brother and constantly reminded him of the importance of their family and culture: to never stray away. He would get beaten and sexually abused when he refused to acknowledge Ottoman teachings. One day, Vlad wanted to visit Radu in his quarters until he saw something strengthening his hatred. Vlad saw Mehmed and Radu having intercourse; the rumors were true. Deep down, he wanted to go in and stop such an atrocious act that was a sin to God.

However, he walked away in anger, hurt, and hatred. Vlad made a vow to God that he would kill the Ottomans.

Slowly, the people in the building began to go to their rooms to rest. Tomorrow, they will all return to Wallachia. Vlad decided to go back to his room and rest for tomorrow. His thoughts then trailed to the young woman, Angelina. He had difficulty believing that she was from a different time. Yet, she did have those objects that he had never seen before.

When returning to his room, Angelina lay on the floor with an empty plate beside her; she was asleep. Was it possible that she was from another time? If so, what was her purpose? Vlad could wake her and force her to answer his questions, but he was exhausted and not in the mood. He wanted to have a peaceful sleep. Vlad undressed until he had his undergarments, got on his bed, and tried to sleep.

Minutes passed, and he was about to close his eyes when he heard Angelina snoring. The snoring was not as loud, and he tried to fall back to sleep, but then her snoring got louder and rougher. Vlad sat up from his bed and looked at the young woman. She was dead asleep, drips of her saliva dripping from her lips. "Woman, quiet yourself."

Angelina was still asleep and still snoring. "Grandma, Grandpa..." The Voivode didn't understand what she was saying but knew that whoever she called out was essential to her. After a few more tears, Saraya eventually calmed down, and her snoring became quiet. Vlad waited a few moments and decided to lay back on his bed, and sleep overtook him.

Eventually, morning arrived, and Angelina was still asleep but woke up when she landed on something hard. When she woke up, she noticed hay. The young woman looked at her surroundings and saw that she was outside. "What the heck is going on?"

"You're finally awake." Vlad was on his horse, fixing his gloves.

"Wh-What's happening?"

"We're all returning to my palace in Wallachia. I told you that you were coming with us. Also..." Vlad looked at her. "You snored like a man last night."

Angelina felt her face turn warm. "I-I don't! I-I-I-"

Vlad let out a humorless chuckle. "In denial, are you? I was about to wake you and force you to be silent, but then you called out 'Grandma' and 'Grandpa,' and you fell asleep."

"Those were my grandparents. I told you they took care of me more than my Mother." Angelina looked away.

Vlad raised an eyebrow and scoffed. He then commanded his horse to ride before his men. "It is time to leave. We return to Wallachia. Let us march."

Everyone began to move and follow their Voivode. Angelina felt nervous. She didn't know what was going to happen to her and if she was going to survive.

Little Amusement

Vlad rode ahead of his people, leading them back to his castle. The road was long but calm, but he couldn't stop thinking about his prisoner. Angelina intrigued him, and he wanted to know more about her.

He enjoyed torturing prisoners to get the whole truth, but Angelina seemed to know about his reputation and hadn't hesitated to be honest. They were almost at Wallachia, and it would take another two hours. It would be an excellent opportunity to speak with her more. He motioned out his hand, and everyone stopped. "We will rest for a moment. Eat, drink, feed the horses, and rest. We will arrive at the palace within two hours." Men and women sighed in relief as many got off their horses and carts or just sat on the floor from walking many miles.

Vlad got off his horse and gave it to one of his men to help feed and water it to prepare for the next part of their journey. He walked back where he saw the cart where Angelina was supposed to be in. Once he arrived, he saw Angelina sleeping soundly, giving off quiet-like snores. Vlad stared at her as he lifted one of his eyebrows. He couldn't believe Angelina would still sleep since it had only been a few hours. "Woman, wake up."

She didn't wake up; she snored in response. Vlad was getting annoyed. Without warning, he grabbed the back of her clothing and dragged her off the cart, making her fall. "Ow, what the hell!?"

"What did you say?"

"In my time, we say that when we are confused, scared, angry, or for humor. It's complicated. Now, what was that for?"

"You snore like a man." He took off his gloves. Comfortable, I presume?"

Angelina turned onto her back while looking at Vlad and the sky. "Very. Did I do something wrong?"

"We are to rest for an hour. We're almost at my castle; I wish to speak with you."

He noticed that her cheeks were turning red. "Umm, I need to pee and poo." Angelina groaned. "I need to relieve myself. We've been on the road for hours. I've been holding it in."

"Ah, I see." He then lifted Angelina by her clothes and undid the ropes of her feet. "I will take you."

"Uh, no, that's not necessary. I-"

He pushed her forward. "I wasn't giving you any ultimatum, woman. I can't have you run away. I'm not as merciful as my men here." He motioned her by large trees and put her behind one of them. He stood by the corner of the tree, giving Angelina privacy."

Angelina couldn't believe she was doing her business close with one of the most prolific serial killers in history. While defecating, Angelina slowly turned behind her and saw Vlad's arm by the corner of the tree. "Hey, I'm not done yet!"

Vlad rolled his eyes at the other end of the tree. "I'm not even looking at you, woman. I have etiquette on respecting a woman's virtue. Only if women respect themselves, of course."

"I-I see. Sorry if I say this, but you are known for being cruel. I could have never imagined you being...well...you know...somewhat respectful."

The silence was between them; Vlad stood by the tree with crossed arms. No one ever said that to him. "There are many things you don't know and wouldn't want to know, woman. I am curious about why you came here to my land."

"Well, I came to this country to explore. I love learning, traveling, and meeting new people. Coming here, you know, at this time. Not so much." A fart escaped. "Oops, sorry about that!"

A chuckle escaped his lips. "I can imagine that. Although, it's difficult for me to believe you are not from this time. I still think you are mad."

Angelina sighed in relief. "Well, you have a right to think what you want. I've tried everything possible to convince you. As I said, I know you have a reputation, sir. Although, I wouldn't be much use to you."

"On the contrary. I believe you will be quite useful. Once we arrive at my castle, I can think of many things I can use you for."

After finishing and cleaning herself with a few napkins in her backpack, she announced that she was done. Vlad walked from the corner of the tree and saw her about to lift her pants. He caught sight of her bottom and private. Vlad said nothing as Angelina got herself ready. He went to her and grabbed her tied hands. "We must return. We will soon be on the road and arrive at my palace. There's also something you need to know."

"Which is?"

"My wife can be something else. You will see once you meet her."

Angelina didn't know why, but she couldn't remove the horrible feeling in her stomach.

Wallachia

V lad and his men kept going forward; it felt like hours for Angelina. However, the roads were less bumpy, and now they were surrounded by more trees. "We're getting close!" a man yelled. Ahead, a castle-like fortress was up on a rocky, grassy hill with the forest beneath. It dawned on Angelina that she was looking at Bran Castle. She almost forgot that the castle was where Vlad lived while facing the Ottomans.

While walking toward the castle, they walked into a village where many people were doing their daily chores. When Vlad and his men arrived, many villagers cheered for the Voivode, and others looked at him with fear. It made her nervous because she didn't know what Vlad was planning for her.

After what felt like an eternity, everyone arrived at the castle's entrance. The guards standing by the castle's walls announced the return of Vlad and his men. The gates were opened, and everyone entered. Through the walls, servants and guards were getting in their formation. Everyone was silent as they were in Vlad's presence. Two stable boys who looked to be in their adolescents went to him. One got the horse reigns, while the other put a small stair for Vlad to step on.

Once he got off his horse, a man with puffy black hair and a short mustache stepped forward. The man had facial hair that looked poorly trimmed, making him look older than his actual age. His eyes were a dull brown with bags under his eyes. The man was a bit thin, but his clothes made it seem as if he was of average weight. Seeing him made it seem as if he was the living dead.

Angelina felt a bit sorry for the man. Being with Vlad was another stress level. The man bowed. "Voivode, you have made a safe return. I presume everything went well?"

"Indeed, Alexandrei. How was everything during my absence?"

"Not too much trouble. Ever since you calmed down the Saxons, there were a few rebels here and there. However, there is no need to fret; they were dealt with accordingly. Yet, I know the biggest threat is the Ottomans, which reminds me. I received another letter from Sultan's council."

Vlad scoffed as Alexandrei gave him the letter. "The scoundrels still ask for tribute. Well, they will soon hear about the slaughter of their men soon enough. How is Minah?"

"She is doing well and is due to give birth any day now. She is in her chambers." Alexandrei then noticed two men walking toward them with another person in tow. "Who is that?"

Vlad turned his head slightly. "Oh, she is a woman that my men found. She was suspected of being with the Ottomans, but she is slowly convincing me she is not. However, I am not finished interrogating her."

"The name is Angelina if you would like to know."

Alexandrei looked at Angelina from head to toe. He was shocked by her clothing and her appearance. "She does look like those savages. Are you certain she is not an enemy?"

"No, I'm American."

Everyone was silent as they watched everything unfold. "What is she speaking of?" Alexandrei slowly walked to Angelina, his eyes never leaving hers. He stood before her even if he looked like a sickly man; the young woman could feel a bit of his intimidation. "Have I asked you to speak, savage?"

Angelina's eyes became wide. "He called me a savage!?" She began to feel angry. "Excuse me?"

"Voivode, it seems that this woman doesn't know her place. I'm surprised you haven't put her head in a spike."

"At least I know how to respect people, estupido (asshole)."

Suddenly, Alexandrei slapped Angelina across the face, and the slap echoed. The slap was painful. Her ear was buzzing. However, she bit her lower lip and slowly looked at the man. "Are you done? All you're doing is proving my point. What have I done to you and you?"

"You dare-!?"

Alexandrei was about to slap her again, but Vlad spoke out. "Enough! Take her to the dungeons and ensure she is not given food or water. I will eventually go and speak to her."

Angelina was forcibly taken away, and everyone watched. "The arrogance in her tone! You let her speak to you in that manner!?"

Voivode glared at him, and Alexandrei became silent. "Worry not; she will be punished accordingly. For now, I will visit my wife." Vlad went inside his palace, and Alexandrei followed.

Minah

Angelina was taken inside the castle and saw the simplicity and beauty of the castle. Servants were working and were on and about. The young woman felt like she was in a fairytale while in the castle.

The guards were taking her further into the castle, but they all stopped when a young woman approached them. The young woman had long black hair but was put in a bun covered with pearls. Her skin was slightly pale as milk, which made her hair shine. She wore a long blue dress with white designs, pearl necklaces, and earrings. The woman had a slightly chubby face. She was also not alone; she also had female servants behind her. Angelina noticed that the young woman was pregnant.

The guards bowed and forcibly hit Angelina's head down.

"Guards, my husband has arrived, I presume?"

"Yes, my Lady Minah. He is to enter soon."

"Who is this? My husband's prisoner?" Angelina realized that the woman in front of her was Vlad's wife. In history, everyone knew about his second wife, but not much was not known about his first wife. She thought it was comical that movies in her era used the name Minah. "Why do you smile, woman? Does it bring you joy to be taken to the dungeons?"

Angelina had the urge to let out an annoyed groan. "Why were rich people in this bigger assholes than in my time?" She sighed. "No, forgive me, my Lady."

The noblewoman eyed her. "You wear strange clothing. It is nothing I have seen before. Where are you from?"

"I'm from another nation. I've come here for travel."

"You jest. You could be a spy to kill my husband."

Footsteps were heard going toward them. "Wife, I see you met my prisoner." Vlad and Alexandrei entered. All bowed to him; Angelina was forced. "Indeed, I have a husband. I am surprised that you haven't killed her yet."

"I agree with Lady Minah. This woman has a vile tongue," said Alexandrei.

Angelina bit her lower lip. "I want to kick his ass so bad," she thought.

Vlad glanced at Angelina. "I am still to decide her fate. For now, she must think of her actions. Take her to the dungeons."

The guards took Angelina down a couple of stairs that led to another part of the castle. Torches dimly lit gave little light in the hallway. Angelina was thrown into a prison cell farther from the rest, and the guards closed and locked the door. She was left alone; the prison was cold. "I must think of a way to get out of here, but now I have to think of ways to survive."

Day turned into night; Vlad and Minah sat in the dining room, where servants prepared their meals. The silence irked Minah as she glanced at her husband occasionally. "I missed you, dear husband. I am happy that you could stop parts of Mehmed's army."

A piece of cheese was eaten; Vlad sighed. "Sultan Mehmed still desires my obedience to him, blasted heathen."

"Husband, I worry about possible attacks on the kingdom. Do you believe it would be wise to ask for more assistance?"

"Do not worry about such things. Your duty is to give birth to my sons, for they will one day rule Wallachia."

The noblewoman noticed her husband's thoughtful gaze. "What will you do with that woman? Alexandrei seems to have a distaste for her."

Vlad chuckled. "She spoke back to him. Alexandrei never had the patience for disobedient women."

"Neither do you, husband. Strangely, you would keep this woman alive."

The Voivode looked at his wife. "I am curious about her. She speaks and dresses differently. She told me things that were hard to believe. That is why I am keeping her alive."

This didn't sit well with Minah. "I see. You are only keeping her alive for mere curiosity?"

"You may be carrying my child, but you know I don't tolerate being questioned, not even by you or any other woman. You know that you can always be replaceable. It would be in your best interest not to question my actions. Remember what happened last time?"

Minah was silent as she watched her husband eat his meal and put her hand over her womb. Vlad chuckled at his wife's reaction. He enjoyed the power he had over her and others. Tomorrow, he would put his idea into motion.

Gaunt

Angelina would doze intermittently and didn't know if it was day or night. Her cell was cold, and it was difficult to sleep properly. "You, woman." The young woman opened her eyes and looked around. She crawled toward the prison bars and saw another cell from afar. She saw a disheveled man, his dark hair trailing down to his chin. His skin was filled with sweat and dirt; his appearance was gaunt, as if malnourished. There were many wrinkles on his face and his hands. However, the man had dark green eyes that flowed in the darkness like emeralds. Even with his gaunt-like appearance, Angelina noticed some handsomeness in his appearance.

"Wh-Who are you?"

"I am Bioan. We all have seen your arrival at the prisons. Why have you been put here?"

Angelina sighed and couldn't help but feel sorry for Bioan. She wondered how long he had been locked away. "I was found in the Hoia-Baciu Forest, and they think I'm an Ottoman spy or something. I'm no spy. I accidentally got lost in the forest; I'm Angelina, by the way."

Bioan nodded as he smiled. "A pleasure. You wear the most unusual clothing. I have never seen such a thing."

"I know, it's a long story. Please believe that I'm not a spy but a traveler."

Bioan raised an eyebrow as he never heard of a female solo traveler. It amazed him that she looked unscathed. "A traveler? It is dangerous for a woman to go on and about to travel alone. Women are most vulnerable and would survive alone in such cruelty."

Angelina wanted to tell him she was from a different era but thought it would complicate things. Vlad was still having a hard time believing her. She thought it would be best to keep it to herself until asked. "I have no family, and it would have been hard alone anyway. I made sure to be careful during my travels. Well, I guess you can say my luck ran out."

"Indeed, I thought that you angered Lady Minah. She can be cruel as Vlad."

"R-Really? I guess misery loves company. I only met her for a moment. She didn't look...evil."

Bioan laid on the prison bars. "You only met her for a moment, but the more you stay, the more you see her true self."

"What about you? What are you in for?"

"I have been wrongfully accused of being with the Ottomans as well. I am but a soldier fighting for God's glory and our Voivode. I have also been under the command of Alexandrei, and he just accused me of something I would not have dared to do and be."

The young woman rolled her eyes when hearing Alexandrei's name. "Oh, you also worked for Alexandrei? I barely met him, and he seems like an ass. He has a bad attitude."

The gaunt-like man let out a small laugh. He has been imprisoned on what seemed like an eternity. It has been a while since he was able to express some sort of laugh, even when he was in the outside world. Bioan glanced at Angelina and couldn't deny that she was a beauty. "Alexandrei is a difficult man to be with. Soldiers dislike him, but he is our Voivode's second in command. We have no choice but to follow his orders if need be."

"I find it bizarre that Alexandrei would just accuse you out of nowhere. There has to be a reason why he would accuse you of being with the Ottomans."

"Indeed, word spread that there is a traitor among us. The Voivode and Alexandrei have been having a watchful eye, especially since there is trouble with the Saxons."

Angelina was about to speak, but then she and Bioan heard the prison door open and a couple of footsteps. Bioan motioned Amgelina to go back and did so. The footsteps were getting closer to her side, and she felt nervous before her cell was Vlad. "Have you slept well?"

"Not much. Is it morning already? Time flies by in here."

"So, I hear. Have you thought about what you have done?"

The young woman was confused. "Oh, is it about Alexandrei? I felt that I did nothing wrong. I was only verbally defending myself."

Vlad raised an eyebrow. "So you refuse to acknowledge your wrongs?"

"No, s-sir. If I have done something wrong, I would admit it without complaint; I refuse to be a hypocrite. I am being accused of being something that I am not. Is it wrong to defend my innocence? You saw my belongings, which you have never seen before. I explained what they are and where they come from. I am no spy, and I never disrespected Alexandrei. I am just a traveler in the wrong place and time."

It was silent for a moment as Vlad contemplated that Angelina brought a good point. When someone lied to him, he would know immediately. Even though Angelina was nervous, her eyes never wavered. "Bring her to the secret chambers." The guards opened the prison doors and forcibly took Angelina out. Vlad walked ahead and went to another entry in the prison that led somewhere else. Once inside, the room was even dimmer with feint fire torches. It was difficult to see, but one guard walked behind Vlad with a fire torch. Angelina heard soft groaning and then saw something in front of her. Her eyes widened as she realized she was in a torture chamber.

The young woman was horrified at seeing men sitting on the spikey chair; others were in an iron maiden. The walls also chained men; their bodies were whipped until they bled. Some had their hands tied and were dangling from the ceiling; the weight of their bodies extending their arms caused excruciating pain. "My god..." The sight of blood was everywhere, like a river of blood.

Vlad turned with a smirk. "Welcome to my little playroom, woman. This is where people disobey or betray." He grabbed Angelina's arm and pushed her onto the floor. Angelina fell into a small pool of blood. When she looked up, her eyes became wider when she saw a young woman who looked to be in her mid-twenties dangling from the ceiling with her hands tied behind her. The woman looked tortured as she was nude with lashes throughout her body.

"This is to show you that no matter if you are a man or woman, all of you are subjected to the same fate. If you lie or disobey, then this will be your consequence." Angelina had the urge to vomit. The tortured people, the stench, and the sight of blood were getting to her. Stand on your feet. You and I will speak in my study. There is much to speak about."

Angelina slowly stood, and two guards grabbed her arms and motioned her out of the chambers. Angelina didn't know what her fate would be.

Voice

Angelina followed Vlad into his study while the other servants stared at her. The young woman didn't know what to expect, and Vlad, knowing his history, could expect the worst. Angelina knew that he was capable of doing anything to keep his power. If she were to survive, she would have to play his game. Eventually, they arrived at Vlad's study, which was decent-sized. It is composed of a wooden desk with a couple of shelves of books and scrolls. Cabinets with pottery and small statues, two windows, and a couple of fire torches lit up the room.

Two chairs were in front of his desk, but Angelina was made to stand by the guards. Vlad stood behind his desk and motioned the guards to leave, leaving the two alone. Angelina looked around. "Y-You have a beautiful study, sir."

Vlad raised an eyebrow. "You are not to speak until spoken to. You will no longer call me 'sir,' but wither Voivode or Lord. Understood?"

"Y-Yes s-I mean, Voivode."

"Now. I still don't trust you, and even though you showed me things, you could still be a threat. You will stay here in my castle and be a servant of my household. You saw the consequences of what happens when I am disobeyed or lied to." A chill ran through Angelina's body and nodded in response. "You say that you're a traveler. Why would a woman travel alone? You wish to be killed or be taken?"

"W-With your permission to speak, V-Voivode. I mentioned to you that I am from another time and country more than four to five hundred years into the future. In my country and time, there are many nations where women can travel with and without company."

This surprised Vlad. "A woman can travel unaccompanied? What abomination is this you speak of?"

Angelina remembered that women in this era didn't have many rights, only women of nobility. She read in history books that Vlad was cruel to not only his enemies and innocent civilians that were men but also women. "I know it is a shock to hear this, but what I tell you is the truth, Voivode. As centuries progress, so do the thoughts and values of people and societies. Many wars happened, but also new laws and technology." Angelina smiled. "We have cars that drive through roads with speed. We have airplanes that fly in the skies to get to different countries within hours."

Vlad raised his right hand, and Angelina stopped talking. "You speak of unruly things." He then got Angelina's bag that was taken and took out more things. "What is this?"

"Oh, it's considered old in my time, but it's called an Apple iPod. In my time, they are out of style, but it comes in handy when there's no wifi. The iPod plays my favorite songs and music. M-May I show you?"

The Voivode nodded, and he let Angelina turn on the iPod, and he was amazed that by simply touching it, it could make turns and do movements. Angelina reached into her bag, and Vlad grabbed her hand. "What are you doing, woman?"

"I wanted to get my earphone to connect it with the iPod. If you want to hear the music to yourself, you use them. Look." She slowly lifted her hands and had the earphones. Vlad let go of her hand and watched her make the connections. "You must put them in your ears to hear the music."

"You think me as a fool."

Angelina sighed and put the earphones in her ears. Vlad heard a slight noise coming from them and saw Angelina smile. "Music always soothes me when I have stress in my life. Here." She motioned the earphones to him. "Do you want to put them on, or should I put them on for you?"

Vlad grabbed them and did what he saw Angelina do. Angelina pushed a button, and then Vlad heard music. He violently flinched as the music went into his ears. Angelina motioned out her hands, telling him to calm down. "Don't worry. Nothing will happen to you. Just listen and be at peace." She pushed the button again. Vlad heard music. He was surprised by the soft and powerful music; the one who sang was a woman. Never had he listened to a woman have a soft yet firm voice. The instruments also made an addicting sound. The combination was astounding.

To his surprise, the music made him feel at ease. The song made him so at ease that he sat on his chair and closed his eyes, listening to the

song. He enjoyed how the woman sang. Eventually, the song ended.
Vlad opened his eyes and looked at Angelina standing, looking at
him. "D-Did you like it? The singer is Tarja Turunen, and her song
is Phantom of the Opera. It's one of my favorites."

https://youtu.be/n1G5WiMoRjw

"I did enjoy it. There is more music in this iPod?"

"Yeah, but the battery runs out, and I would have to charge it, but
there are no plugs here. So we shouldn't use it entirely."

Vlad was silent for a moment and took off the earphones. "I desire to
know more of your supposed time and listen to more of this iPod.
You have much more to prove, so I have thought of a solution." He
stood as he put the iPod down on his desk. "You will be one of my
wife's lady-in-waiting. You will tend to and watch over her needs
since she carries our child. You will inform me about her well-being.
Also, you will become my mistress."

Angelina's eyes became wide. "E-Excuse me? Y-Your mistress?"

"It is as you heard. Since my wife is with child, I still have to tend to
my needs. My wife will have no say in my decision."

She couldn't believe her ears. He wanted her to become his pleasure tool. "What happens if I don't want to become your mistress? I don't want to betray the woman I would be working for."

Vlad's expression became serious. "You have no say or have the right to disobey my orders. I do not like having my orders disobeyed."

"I know, but I have morals, respect for others, and my self-respect, Voivode. I cannot give my body to a man I have no feelings for or hold no feelings for me. Nonetheless, have respect for me. If I am to give myself to a man, it would be out of love and respect."

Vlad was quiet and then chuckled. "Interesting. You refuse my offer because you would rather have your honor and self-respect. You are different from my other mistresses. Well, you will soon change your mind. You will still work for my wife and sleep with the female servants. You and I will meet here again tomorrow night. "Guards!" The guards entered. "Take her to the female servant quarters."

The guard took Angelina out of his study, leaving him alone. Vlad sat back on his chair, put the earphones on, and played the song again.

Women

Angelina was taken to the female servant quarters on one of the lower floors. It was not as low as the prisons. Once they arrived in front of the door, the guards let her go and motioned her to go inside. "Don't get any ideas of trying to escape. We guard the castle all night. You know the punishment if you try," said one of the guards.

"Yeah, I saw." She slowly opened the door. Once opened, she peaked inside, and there were rows of beds with women inside. Many women were either bathing, changing, brushing their hair, or were on their beds. Angelina slowly entered, closing the door behind her. No one noticed her, and it made her nervous. She gathered her courage. "H-Hello. I-I was ordered to come here."

Everyone stopped what they were doing and finally noticed Angelina. Some of the women were silent while others whispered among one another. Suddenly an older woman walked before Angelin and stopped giving them space. The woman had messy black hair with many gray hairs. She was small in stature than Angelina. Her eyes were dark brown and had some bags beneath. The older woman had many wrinkles on her face. She was slightly overweight. Angelina noticed the woman also had a scar on her neck and a mole on the right side of her nose. "So you are the new woman that everyone speaks about." The older woman eyed Angelina from head to toe. "You wear such strange clothing that we haven't seen before. What is your name?"

"Angelina. It's nice to meet you..."

"Ioana. I am the main lady-in-waiting for Lady Minah and in charge of her household. The Voivode ordered you to be a part of the female servants."

"Yes, madam. He also told me that I am to be one of...Lady Minah's ladies-in-waiting."

The women whispered to one another while Ioana raised an eyebrow. "The Voivode wouldn't just choose any woman to be in his wife's household."

"I-I understand. Believe me that I didn't want any part of this. I was taken against my will."

"Really. You look like a mere peasant," laughed one of the women.

Angelina felt angered as she looked at the young woman. She had long brunette hair that was wet from her bath. Her skin was slightly pale, with many freckles on her face, shoulders, and back. Her lips were slightly discolored from the dryness; her teeth were crooked and yellow. She had a little muffin top. "You can say that, I guess. We would be here working for the cruel rich if we weren't, right?"

She received many glares, but Angelina went through a lot in the last couple of days and hours. All she wanted was to sleep. "That is enough of you, Daciana. I will speak to Lady Minah, and if all goes well, be trained in your duties. Follow me." The young woman followed Ioana to the left corner of the room, with an empty bed. It was small, but Angelina didn't care. All she cared about was rest. "I will give you your clothing to sleep in and what you will wear when working in Lady Minah's quarters." Angelina sat on the bed and took off her shoes as Ioana went off.

She was still receiving some stares and noticed that the young woman next to her was sitting on her bed. The young woman had brunette hair, light brown eyes, and light olive skin with scars on her chest. She had acne on her face and a slightly long nose; she had an average appearance. Angelina thought that she had a somewhat youthful appearance, but the stress made her look older than she was."You wear strange clothes. I'm surprised that our Voicode didn't kill you. You look like an Ottoman."

"I get that a lot. You know, you look young to work here."

"I am sixteen and have been a servant all my life. My mother was a servant before me, so you can say that it is in the family. I am Sorina. You are Angelina, right?"

"Y-Yeah." Angelina motioned out her hand toward Sorina. Sorina looked at her hand and looked confused. "Where I'm from, we shake hands to greet one another. It's a sign of respect." Sorina slowly held onto her hand, and Angelina motioned up and down. They let go.

"What a strange custom. Where are you from? From the looks of it, you are not from here."

Angelina noticed many of the women looking at them; they were curious. She thought about telling them the truth. However, she felt hesitation. Vlad was still cautious of her and felt that telling Sorina about her timeline could create more problems. She and the others would view her as insane. The young woman didn't want any more problems. "Well, would you believe me that I am not from this country? I have crossed the oceans to get here."

"Impossible! We are not close to the waters! How were you able to cross the waters?" asked one of the women.

Most of the women were curious about Angelina's origins, and she knew. "It would sound impossible, but it's not. My mother and father abandoned me, and my grandparents cared for me. However, they both died of illness, and I have been alone since then. However, I refused to succumb to my fate and became a traveler. My goal is to write books of my travels, but as you know, here I am."

Ioana returned with a small pile of clothing. "I got you clothing that looks to be your size. Do not lose them; you are responsible for keeping them clean. You will wake up early to meet Lady Minah. It is time to sleep, all of you!"

The women were finishing what they were doing before going to bed. Angelina got off her modern clothing and into a plain dark beige dress. "Will you tell us stories tomorrow night? I am intrigued by your travels."

"Uh, sure. I have many stories to tell."

Duties

"It is dawn, time to wake up!" announced Ioana.

Angelina woke up from her slumber as she stretched. When she woke up, her body felt sore. Her eyes were still groggy. However, Angelina sat up from the bed as she saw the rest of the women immediately getting off their beds and preparing themselves for the day.

"Good morning, Angelina. You must get yourself ready; Ioana disapproves of laziness." Sorina looked back and forth. "You might end up punished for not doing your duties well."

Angelina got off the bed and began to make it. Once finished, she dressed in the clothing that Ioana had given her the day before. She felt bizarre wearing the clothes of the past. However, she also felt curious since she had the opportunity to experience what people wore, ate, and lived in the past. She stood by the bed as she watched the other women preparing themselves. "Would you like me to brush your hair? Lady Minah doesn't like it when servants' strands of hair fall in her quarters."

"Uh, sure. My hair can be complicated."

Sorina shrugged her shoulders. "I do like a challenge." The teen motioned Angelina to sit on a wooden chair as she got a wooden comb and water. Sorina began to brush her hair and felt that many parts of her hair were tangled. "You haven't brushed your hair in a while."

"Well, let's say I had quite an adventure that I didn't have the time to take care of myself." The two were silent momentarily. "Sorina, how is it working for Lady Minah?"

The adolescent stopped brushing her hair as she put in some water. "She can be...difficult at times. You can say that Lady Minah loves perfection. She is not afraid to punish her servants for a mere error."

It was as Angelina feared; Minah was as cruel as her husband. Surprisingly she couldn't entirely fault the noblewoman; her husband didn't have the greatest reputation. "H-Have you ever been punished?"

Sorina stilled for a few seconds but then tied Angelina's hair in a bun. "Many times. I will show you how to do your duties. I am certain that Lady Minah will allow you to receive your education on how to serve her well. You're ready."

"Thank you, Sorina. I think you and I will become good friends."

"Friends, eh? Yet, you are older than I."

Angelina shrugged her shoulders. "Well, times have changed. Besides, at times like these, one needs at least a friend to survive."

"I guess you're right, but now we must have breakfast. I will show you the kitchen." All the women walked out of the quarters and through the halls toward a kitchen where many servants were cooking or eating. On the tables were plates and bowls of bread, meats, cheese, and fruits. Angelina felt her stomach growl with hunger. She followed Sorina's lead, and the two got their plates of food. "We must always eat in a hurry; the Lords and Ladies will soon wake."

The young woman noticed how everyone was quickly eating their breakfast. The food was decent, but Angelina thought most of the food lacked flavor. She couldn't complain since she had traveled to the past. However, she and everyone finished their food and left the dishes to the kitchen workers. Ioana stood by the exit as the female servants stood before her. "Remember your duties well. Lady Minah is with child, and she requires more care." She looked at Angelina and motioned her to come to her. "I will introduce you to Lady Minah. You are to bow to her and not look at her in the face until ordered. Whatever she orders, you must do. Understand?"

"Yeah."

"Everyone, to your duties. Sorina, make certain to bring Lady Minah's breakfast. Let's go." Many women followed Ioana, while others went to other parts of the castle. The ladies-in-waiting walked up many stairs until they reached the castle's upper part. They got to a nicely decorated part of the castle with portraits, banners, and other statues. The ladies stopped in front of a large wooden door; Ioana walked ahead and gently knocked on the door. "Lady Minah, it is morning."

It was silent for a few seconds until everyone heard a faint response. "Enter."

Ioana opened the door and entered first; the rest followed suit. Once inside, Ioana motioned Angelina to stand by the door while the ladies-in-waiting opened the curtains and prepared the clothing, jewelry, and hair utensils.

Minah was still lying on her bed as she stretched out her arms and slowly sat up from her bed. "Lady Minah, we bid you good morning." Ioana and the ladies-in-waiting bowed. Sorina put the tray of food on the beautifully decorated table. Minah stood and went to eat her breakfast. As she sat, Minah noticed Angelina. "Why is she here?"

All were silent and stood behind the noblewoman. Sorina looked at Angelina and slightly nodded, telling her to remain calm. Ioana motioned Angelina to walk forward, but she stopped to have space between her and the noblewoman. The young woman bowed but did not look Minah straight in the face. "My Lady, our Voivode ordered her to be one of your ladies-in-waiting."

Minah looked displeased. "Yet, he suspects her as a spy and wants her under my wing. My husband has truly lost his mind. Look at me." The young woman slowly lifted her head and looked at Minah. "What is your name again?"

"Angelina, my Lady. I promise to work hard for you."

The room was silent; only the echoes of men outside were heard. "I do not and will not trust you until my husband says so. I expect nothing but the best from my servants. Any wrongdoing, and I will hesitate to have you punished. Do you understand?"

"Yes, my Lady."

"Lady Minah, I decided to have Sorina teach her of her duties to serve you. She-"

Minah motioned out her hand. "She will learn on her own. Everyone here learned on her own, and so will she. She will learn the easy and hard way. After finishing my breakfast, I want my bath drawn." She looked at Angelina. "You are to go and prepare my bath."

"Wh-Where is your bath located so I may prepare it for you?" Angelina saw Sorina mouthing out 'next door.' She smiled. "Never mind, I will figure it out on my own. Enjoy your breakfast, my Lady." Angelina walked out of the room and to the next room, where there was a large wooden tub with a fireplace, bathing materials, and more. She knew that she had to warm the water up, and to her luck, the fireplace was on. All she had to do was warm the water up. "This will probably be one of my worst jobs ever."

Ease

Angelina had never felt so miserable; Minah was worse than anticipated. The noblewoman was rude and spoiled, with a terrible temper. She made many demands from her ladies-in-waiting but went after Angelina the most. Angelina was given the worst duties, such as cleaning after her many pets, which consisted of ten dogs, fifteen birds, and two horses. When she or another lady-in-waiting made mistakes, they were beaten with a rod.

She wanted to fight back but would have to bite her tongue. Angelina was no longer in her time, and since Minah was Vlad's wife, nothing could be done. It was night, and Minah was being prepared to go to bed. She wore a beautiful white nightgown; her pregnant belly was noticeable. Angelina watched as Sorina undoing Minah's braids;

Minah looked at Angelina through the mirror. "You have made many mistakes working for me; I shall tell my husband."

"Go ahead, you damn wench! I would rather be put to prison than work for another instant!" Angelina thought to herself. However, she couldn't break character, or else she would get another beating. "As you wish, my lady."

Angelina motioned Sorina to stop. Sorina, on the other hand, glanced at Angelina as if telling her that her answer was incorrect. "The noblewoman slowly turned to face her and noticed that Angelina had her hands together while looking down at the ground. "You will not beg for mercy, servant? My husband will not be pleased to hear that a servant hasn't been up to standard."

"No, my Lady. I know I have not met your standards, and I do not want to cause you even more disappointment. I will accept my fate, even death."

The ladies-in-waiting glanced at her; Sorina was shocked at what her new friend said but couldn't help but admire her courage. Minah bit her lower lip. "Very well, if that is what you want, expect your punishment tomorrow. Leave."

The young woman bowed and left her room. While out and far from view, Angelina lay by the wall but flinched when she felt a sting from her scars. She knew that Minah was angered, but Angelina couldn't help but feel a sense of pride for not lowering so low as to beg. "Angelina," said a feminine voice.

Angelina let out a quiet-like squeal. "Oh, Ioana. S-Sorry, I did not see you. I-"

"The Voivode wishes to speak with you in his study; follow me."

Neither woman said anything to the other; Angelina felt her heart beating rapidly. "Ioana probably told him how poorly I was doing!"

Ioana stopped and slowly turned to her. "I have witnessed your many mistakes throughout the day, and I had to speak to the Voivode since he ordered me to keep an eye on you and to report to him."

"I understand, Ioana. I need to prepare whatever is coming to me."

The older woman sighed as she crossed her arms. "If you expect a grueling punishment, rest assured that it will not happen. You see, our Voivode knew that this was going to happen." This surprised the young woman, who felt at ease; her legs quivered momentarily. "I know Lady Minah is troublesome to work for; I heard what was said before finding you. I do not know if you are plain brave or reckless. Lady Minah loves to inflict pain on women she views as threats."

"She views me as a threat? Why? I don't want to bring harm to anyone."

Ioana cleared her throat. "Come on along. We mustn't let our Voivode wait any longer." The women arrived at the top level of the castle, where they stood before the door. "Once finished with your meeting, rest at the servant's quarters; I will tell Sorina to help you with your bath. Ioana left Angelina alone.

Angelina took a deep breath and tried to regain her composure; she knocked on the door. "Enter." She slowly opened the door and peeked inside; Vlad was writing before his desk. He didn't look up as Angelina entered his study. She closed the door and slowly approached him but stopped midway, leaving a distance between them. "I heard what happened; how was it?" Vlad asked while chuckling.

This made Angelina feel annoyed, making her squeeze her hands together. "I think you know. If I have to be honest, you have a sick sense of humor." This made Vlad stop writing as he slowly looked at her. She felt her skin crawl as his beautiful blue eyes made her uneasy.

"S-Sorry if I offended you, but y-you gave indications that you knew how your wife was going to treat me; you even think it is funny."

Vlad laughed humorlessly while standing from his seat and slowly approaching her. He stood before her; Angelina felt his hot breaths on her head. Never in her life has she felt intimidated by such a man. His laughs stopped; his smile died down. "Whether or not I knew, you should hold your tongue, woman. I have no hesitation in silencing a woman if they speak such words to me."

"I-I know and s-sorry about that. It's just that...I have never done something like this before. I also have never been treated like this." Vlad's stare never dissipated; he noticed slight blood on the back of her dress. Vlad knew that his wife had beaten her. "I wanted to let you know that your wife might tell you of my failings. Please know that I tried my best to do what was asked of me."

The Voivode eventually returned to his seat; it was noticed that he took out her bag and then her phone. "The reason I called you here is for you to show me more of how this thing works. I have been hearing the same song repeatedly, but it got tiresome. Also, a noise has been coming from it." He motioned to come forward while motioning out the phone.

"He called for me just to show him more of my phone? Unbeliev-able!" The young woman got the phone and realized that the battery was low. "The battery is dying because of the constant usage. I need to charge it; I have a wireless charger that might last longer. I need to get it out of my backpack." She motioned out her hand, but Vlad didn't hand her the bag. "I won't do anything rash; I don't have anything that will put you at risk. If the phone is not charged, then it will no longer work. You do want to know more of this, don't you?" Eventually, Vlad handed her her backpack, and Angelina opened one of the front pockets, got out her charger, and plugged it into her phone. "You need to let it charged until it gets to a hundred percent."

"Show me more of this, woman."

"There is no internet connection here. Internet is when data is sent from certain towers; it's complicated. However, there are game apps that you can play. Let me show you." Angelina showed him angry birds and how to play. She couldn't help but notice how intrigued he looked. "Now you try." Vlad did as he observed, and at the beginning, he was doing poorly, but with his determination and pride, he got the hang of it. Angelina watched quietly and couldn't help but notice that his once tense body fell at ease. "C-Can I leave? It seems that you are enjoying yourself."

Vlad stopped playing and gave her his attention. "Yes, and worry not for my wife. Her pregnancy is affecting her mind. You will still work for her. Now you may go." Angelina merely nodded as she walked out of his study, and as she closed the door, she couldn't help but hear the sounds of the game and his chuckles.

"Now, this might work." She went to the servant quarters, thinking about how her phone and Vlad's curiosity about her life might help her survive.

Story

Angelina finally arrived at the female servant quarters, where the women finished dressing or brushing their hair. Upon her arrival, the women looked at her. As Angelina walked toward her bed, Sorina noticed and immediately went to her. "I was worried about you. We heard that you met with the Voivode. W-Were you punished!? Were you cast out!? Please don't tell me that you are to be-!?"

"Sorina, relax. I will still be a lady-in-waiting for Lady Minah. I was just warned to be careful with my words, that's all."

The women mumbled to one another while Sorina motioned Angelina to her bed. "Praise be to our Lord that you were given a chance of life. Our Voivode is not so merciful to those who anger him and

Lady Minah. He usually lets Lady Minha do what she wants with the servants."

"Well, I was fortunate not to have such a fate. Anyway, I need to bathe. It has been a long day, and tomorrow might get worse."

"I'll help you with your bath." The two women went to one of the corners of the quarters, where Sorina warmed some water and put it on the wooden tub covered in white sheets. Angelina still felt a little of being naked with other women, but the others seemed to be used to seeing one another nude. Sorina noticed her uncomfort and got a long white sheet shielding her from view. Angelina unclothed herself as she went inside the tub with warm water. Her body became relaxed in the comfort of the warm waters. When her body was engulfed, Sorina put down the sheet and assisted Angelina with wetting and brushing her hair. "Angelina, you promised to tell me some stories of your travels."

Angelina laid her head on the corner of the tub while Sorina washed her hair. She knew Sorina and the others wouldn't believe her story about the forest; she didn't want to be seen as insane. However, Angelina knew Sorina wouldn't leave her alone until she told a story. "Okay, let me see..." Many women got onto their beds as they looked at Angelina; they were also curious. That was when Angelina remembered one of her trips to Mexico as she went to Merida; it had a lot of beautiful history and scenery. "In one of my travels, I traveled to a country close to the ocean. Many small and big buildings and many towns lived close to the ocean. I have also explored many magnificent caves."

"Caves?"

"Yeah, caves are something that is carved in mountains or stone. Small caves can have nothing but rocks; some have hidden lakes and rivers. Also, I have seen some caves that lead to many paths, some long, some short, and some so tight that one could get stuck in them." It wasn't a total lie; Angelina has been to Mexico a few times since it was affordable, but it held so much beauty even with its bloody history and reputation."

Many women looked intrigued as they listened to her stories. Angelina couldn't deny that she was enjoying having her stories being heard. "There is also a frightful legend about a ghost woman who said she lived. There are many versions of this legend, but the one I heard is that this woman, Maria, was considered beautiful in the village she was from and had many suitors. However, she fell in love with one man in particular."

Sorina was intrigued by the story as she finished washing Angelina's hair with certain herbs. "What then?"

"Well, this man was known to be a womanizer and tried to woo her, but Maria played hard to get, which made him desire her even more. So much so that he asked her to marry him; she accepted. At the beginning of their marriage, they were happy and had two children. However, after a few years, Maria's husband's mind began astray, and he missed his bachelor life." The women were glued to the story as they listened silently, waiting for what would happen next. "Maria's husband fell into his temptations, and he began to have many affairs. Maria found out and begged her husband to think of their family; he didn't change his old ways."

"That is awful! This man has a beautiful wife and still goes after others! What next!?" Sorina washed Angelina's hair with water.

"Maria's husband didn't listen to his wife's pleas and still had affairs. However, he held more love for his children than she. This made Maria go into despair and rage. Rage that her husband would be with other women and love their children more than her. That is when she did the unthinkable; she took her children to a river and drowned them to death."

Many of the women and Sorina gasped in horror. "What, she drowned her poor innocent children!? They have done nothing!" exclaimed one of the women.

Angelina looked at Sorina and nodded. Sorina covered her with a white sheet and helped Angelina with her clothing. Everyone was silent as they waited for her to finish dressing. Once finished, Angelina sat on her bed; Sorina sat beside her and helped brush her hair. "Yes, I agree. The legend is still not finished. "Once her anger subsided, Maria realized what she had done. Grief and guilt overwhelmed her, and she killed herself."

"One sin after another! What horrible crimes!"

"When dead, Maria walked to heaven's gates, but God was repulsed by her actions and sent her to purgatory on Earth to find her children. It is said that Maria would not go to heaven until she found her children. However, since she was to roam in purgatory, legends say that her spirit travels to the rivers at night to find her missing children.

People have said to hear her wails calling for her children, which is why they call her the Wailing Woman. Parents warn their children never to go to the rivers at night; if they do, the Wailing Woman will drown them and take their souls."

"That is dreadful! Do you think the Wailing Woman comes here?" asked Sorina.

"Don't be ridiculous; it's just a stupid story that this woman made!"

All the women looked in one direction. Angelina also noticed her and remembered Ioana mentioning her before. "I was just asking Daciana. Either way, it was a good story; it excited us."

"Hm! It wasn't even that exciting; it happens in life most of the time."

"You are just jealous that she made it out unscathed by the Voivode. Just accept that he desires you no more. He has Lady Minah and will never fall for us, mere servants!"

Angelina could feel the tension and didn't want it to escalate further. "Come no, that's enough. Besides, we all need to sleep since tomorrow we have lots of work. Maybe I will tell you all a different story next time."

Many of the women mumbled as they got ready for bed. Daciana and Sorina glared at one another until Sorina went to her bed. "That legend was well said. I will try to help you more when I can."

"Thank you, it would be much appreciated. Before Angelina laid down to sleep, Daciana gave her an evil glare. Angelina lay down and knew that she and Daciana may not get along.

Preparation

The sun was slowly rising in the skies, and some of its rays hit the castle and went through a particular window. Vlad felt the warmth of the sun's rays, and it woke him up. His light blue eyes shined with the sun, but he immediately covered them and moved to the left side of his bed to escape the light. As he lay on one side of his body, he saw the 'phone' he left on his bed. Vlad couldn't help but admit that he enjoyed using the contraption. For something so small, it brought him much entertainment that he hadn't had in years.

However, the Voivode couldn't remember when he had actual enjoyment or happiness. Ever since childhood, the only one who brought him happiness was his beloved mother, Cneajna. He remembered his mother's dark brown hair and beautiful blue eyes that he had inherited from her. She was a beauty with a beautiful heart who always tried to shield her sons from the violence inside and outside their lives. Vlad also remembered his older brother, Mircea II, whom the family and the people loved. As a child, Vlad always respected his older brother, who was against their father's ideas to join the Ottomans. He was against having him and their brother Radu be sent as prisoners; Mircea was overruled.

Vlad remembered his mother's cries and screams when they took him and Radu away from her. The brothers were taken away from their father's orders due to his mistake of breaking the treaty with the Ottomans.

A burning rage came up in his chest from the memory of his father, a man whom he despised with a consuming passion. A man who loved his pride and power more than his own family. His father, Vlad II Dracul, tried fighting for the throne of Wallachia and asked the Sultan for support. In return, their father gave him and Radu to be hostages to Sultan Mehmed II, where the boys were taught many languages, horseman riding, and, more importantly, Islam. Vlad refused the teachings of the Ottomans and refused to betray his faith; his mother always taught him that their God was the only one and would always be there to guide them. He took the teaching to heart and endured many punishments. However, when Vlad was in his adolescence, he learned of his father's and brother's murder; his mother committed suicide out of fear of being raped and killed in a deplorable manner.

Even though the Ottomans helped him regain the throne when his father and brother were killed, he still hated the Ottomans and his father. He hated how his younger brother Radu accepted the Ottoman way of life. There were times when Vlad lost the throne, but he still was able to regain it in the most brutal ways. He was able to get rid of the Saxons, but now the Ottomans were his biggest enemy.

His thoughts were interrupted when there was a knock on the door. "Voivode, we have arrived with your clothing for the day."

Vlad sat up and permitted the servants to enter his chambers. There were four men with clothing in their hands. Vlad picked a particular outfit and was assisted in changing. While finishing, another male servant, who stood outside, entered. "Voivode, Lord Alexandrei wishes to speak with you."

"Let him enter."

Alexandrei entered the room and bowed to Vlad. "Good morning, Voivode. I hope you had a good slumber."

"Indeed, I have. It has been a while since I had good sleep."

"I see. I am certain you are aware what day it is."

The servants had just finished dressing him and left the two men alone, closing the door behind them. "Indeed. We have found the actual nobles and traitors that helped dispose of your father, and they have been invited for dinner."

Vlad smirked as he looked at himself in the mirror. "Good, everything must go perfect today. I have waited for this moment to have those traitors pay for helping dispose of my brother and father, driving my mother to take her own life."

"I shall inform the servants to make the dinner to your standards and I also have ordered the torturers to get everything ready."

"Good, I shall trust you with that responsibility."

Alexandrei was about to leave but noticed that phone on the bed. "What is that thing, Voivode? I have never seen such a thing."

Vlad forgot to put the phone away. He didn't want anyone to know about it or consider taking it. He had grown fond of the object since it intrigued him so. "It belongs to that woman. I made her a lady-in-waiting for Minah."

"That woman still lives!? You let her live after such disrespect that she has done to me!?"

The Voivode slowly glared at Alexandrei and slowly walked toward him. Alexandrei could feel his Lord's rage by looking at his eyes and looking down on the floor. "Forgive me, Voivode. I know I have spoken out of tongue, but I have said this because of the woman's disrespect."

"I have my reasons, Alexandrei. I have found that woman to be useful and I have a feeling that she will be more of use to me. Again, careful how you display your words at me or I will have your tongue ripped out and have it fed to the pigs. Am I understood?"

"Yes, Voivode. Forgive my impertinence."

"You are forgiven, for now. Now, make sure that everything will be ready."

Alexandrei immediately walked out, and Vlad immediately got the phone and put it in one of the many cabinets in his chambers. There was another knock on the door, and he permitted whoever it was.

Ioana entered and bowed. "Voivode, good morning."

"Ah, Ioana, good morning. You have news about that woman, I trust."

"Well, it is not much since you wish to know of her and her behavior. Last night, she intrigued the other female servants with a story."

This made Vlad raise an eyebrow. "A story?"

"I have heard parts of it, and I was about to stop it, but I couldn't help but be intrigued as well. She has gotten the interest of the other women, except for Daciana, of course."

He wasn't surprised that Daciana may have disdain for Angelina. Vlad took her as his mistress but grew bored of her when she began to ask for something more; she wanted marriage. He laughed at her stupidity. Never in a lifetime would he ask a mere, unattractive peasant for marriage. He tossed her away and threatened to have her tortured to death if she spoke more of the topic; it kept her shut. "Interesting, so she is also a storyteller. Perhaps I can use her for tonight's dinner. She can tell a story to make the guests more comfortable before knowing their fates."

Ioana felt a chill go down her spine. She couldn't believe that she had forgotten about tonight's dinner in the castle in the castle. However, it was the aftermath that was going to happen to the invitees. She failed to inform Angelina of today's activities and knew the young woman was unprepared or did not have the heart to see such atrocities. "A-Are you certain that is wide, Voivode? She is still new and-"

"I have decided that she will be tonight's storyteller. Tell her to think of a story, and do not tell her the true reason. Understood?"

"Yes, Voivode. I shall leave to wake the servants to serve Lady Minah." Ioana left to fulfill her duties but couldn't help but feel terrible about what was to come.

Little Warning

The castle was bustling with servants early in the morning since they were ordered to wake to finish preparing for the festivities. The female servants woke up at their usual time, but some were instructed to help the men prepare while Minah's ladies-in-waiting had to be by their mistress's side. Angelina was surprised to hear that there would be festivities in the castle. Something about it made her feel excited. Although she was made a servant, watching the festivities made her feel at ease. While helping Sorina tie her dress from the back, she saw Ioana walking toward her. "Oh, good morning, Ioana. I promise that I will try to please Lady Minah today and-"

"I need to speak to you in private; follow me to my chambers." Angelina and Sorina looked confused, but Angelina followed her elder to the chamber. Once inside, Ioana closed the door behind her.

Inside her room was a full-sized bed with one cabinet, one mirror, and some wooden boxes with clothes. It was a small room that looked comfortable since it gave Ioana privacy. "I brought you here because the Voivode had given me orders regarding you. For tonight's festivities, you are to be the storyteller."

This surprised Angelina; Vlad wanted her to be the storyteller for the festivities. The more she thought about it, the more she wondered how Vlad knew about her storytelling. The young woman looked at Ioana and wondered if Ioana was keeping an eye on her. It didn't upset her because Ioana didn't have much of a choice, or the consequences would have been dire. "Is he sure that I should be the storyteller? I mean, I believe there are other people that have more experience than I do."

"It is his order, and we mustn't go against it. With that in mind, I would like you to think of a couple stories and you will not work with us."

"A-Are you sure? Did Vlad make such an order?"

Ioana eyed her with sternness. "You will not speak of his name. Remember to call him Voivode since he is our Prince. If the wrong person hears you say his name so casually, they will not hesitate to make you an enemy." Even though she had not known Angelina long, she could tell the young woman had a good soul. It was something rare in such a turbulent time. "To answer your question, he did not. I want you to have some time to get some ideas, but afterward, I want you to work in the great hall to help with the preparations. Worry not; Lady Minah will not dare say anything since our Voivode seems fond of you." Angelina was surprised by Ioana's bluntness. However, she couldn't help but shiver when Ioana mentioned Vlad's fondness for her. Angelina felt it was the opposite and that Vlad was using his power to get what he wanted; he terrified her. "I understand that you don't think as such, but I have never seen our Voivode give much thought to a female servant, not even Daciana. All I will say is be careful of your surroundings. Understand?"

"Yes, ma'am."

The women walked out of the room where the female servants walked out of the servants' quarters and toward their duties. When everyone left, Angelina sat on her bed, contemplating what story she should tell. Last night, she told a horror story, but now that she was in a horrifying era, she didn't want the story to be so negative. However,

Angelina wanted the story to be exciting and full of anticipation. The thought of doing public speaking in an important festivity made her feel pressured not to make mistakes. "I won't be able to think of anything if I sit here and do nothing." Angelina decided to walk toward the great hall. The more she walked, the more she realized she was lost and didn't know where it was.

"It seems you are lost. Need assistance?" said a slightly frail masculine voice.

Angelina stopped as she recognized the voice; she turned around. "It-It's you, Bioan, right?"

"You remember. Yes, it is I. I thought I would not see you again because I feared that the Voivode has done something to you."

"I am glad to see you are okay. Were you found innocent?"

Bioan walked closer to her but still kept his distance. "My life was spared since there was no evidence that I was a spy. I am a mere soldier born to a family of farmers. I was given the position of a mere servant, and I am no longer a soldier. I am certain I am here to be spied upon." He cleared his throat. "Forgive me. I shouldn't have been too bold. I know there are eyes everywhere, and we must be careful of what we speak of."

Angelina nodded. "Well, I'm glad you are well. I am looking for the great hall since I need to help prepare for some festivities." She noticed how quiet Bioan became; he looked grim. "I will take you there." The two walked quietly toward the great hall, and when they got closer, they saw many people going in and out with decorations, candles, and other cleaning objects. "I guess I am here. Thanks, Bioan. Will you be here for the festivities?"

This made him look confused. "Only a selective of servants are allowed to be in the festivities; it is usually the servants with higher ranks. Are you going to serve in the festivities?"

"The...Voivode, said that he wants me to be a storyteller during the festivities so, I am."

Bioan was silent, and just when he was about to speak, another male servant called out to him to help them bring in the wooden crates. "I must leave, and I hope to see one another soon. Also, be careful. Once you are finished with your duty, go as fast as you can." He walked away to help other male servants, leaving a confused Angelina wondering what he meant.

www.ingramcontent.com/pod-product-compliance
Lightning Source LLC
Chambersburg PA
CBHW070411200726
48294CB00003B/1159